KT-520-072

EAST FINCHI
LIBRA

NOODLE the DOODLE

Wins the Day

Jonathan Meres

With illustrations by
Katy Halford

30131 05807486 2

LONDON BOROUGH OF BARNET

This one's for Pablo again. My very own therapet.

First published in 2022 in Great Britain by
Barrington Stoke Ltd
18 Walker Street, Edinburgh, EH3 7LP

www.barringtonstoke.co.uk

Text © 2022 Jonathan Meres
Illustrations © 2022 Katy Halford

The moral right of Jonathan Meres and Katy Halford to be
identified as the author and illustrator of this work has been
asserted in accordance with the Copyright, Designs and
Patents Act, 1988

All rights reserved. No part of this publication may be
reproduced in whole or in any part in any form without the
written permission of the publisher

A CIP catalogue record for this book is available
from the British Library upon request

ISBN: 978-1-80090-109-4

Printed by Hussar Books, Poland

CONTENTS

CHAPTER 1
Exciting News

It was warm and sunny. The sky was blue. Flowers were blooming. Birds were singing and bees were buzzing. Summer was on its way. But at Wigley Primary it was just another Thursday.

"Good morning, everyone!" said Mr Reed.

"Goooood moooooorning, Mis-ter Reeeeeed!" sang all the children together. They stretched out each word like they always did.

"WOOF!" said Noodle the doodle. "WOOF! WOOF! WOOF!"

Noodle was sitting next to Samir.

"What's that, Noodle?" said Mr Reed. "Did you say I've got some exciting news to tell everyone?"

"WOOF!" said Noodle. His tail began wagging like a windscreen wiper.

The children laughed. They liked it when Mr Reed pretended to understand what Noodle was saying. And they liked it when Mr Reed had exciting news too.

"What is it, Mr Reed?" said Lou.

Sol grinned. "Is it your birthday?" he said.

"No, Sol!" laughed Mr Reed. "It's not my birthday!"

Abdul turned to Sol. "You *always* say that, Sol!" he said.

"Yes," said Nora. "But one of these days he'll be right."

"Any other guesses?" said Mr Reed.

"Is it macaroni cheese for lunch, Mr Reed?" said Shakira.

Mr Reed smiled. He knew that Shakira would ask that. Because there was nothing she liked better than macaroni cheese.

"No, Shakira," said Mr Reed. "It's not macaroni cheese. Sorry."

"Oh," said Shakira. She sounded disappointed.

"It's baked potatoes!" said Josh. "It's *always* baked potatoes on Thursday!"

"You should know that, Shakira," said Callum. "Your mum's the school cook!"

"Oh yeah!" said Shakira. "I forgot!"

Sol grinned. "You forgot your mum's the cook?" he said.

"No!" laughed Shakira. "I forgot it was Thursday!"

"Anyone else like to guess what the news might be?" said Mr Reed.

Everyone looked at Mr Reed. They all shook their heads. They wished Mr Reed would hurry up and tell them.

"It's Sports Day next Friday," said Mr Reed.

"YEEEEEEEEEEEEAAAAAAAAAAH!" sang everyone in Mr Reed's class.

Well, *nearly* everyone. Sol didn't join in. He had just remembered something. Something that had happened at a Sports Day when he was very young.

He had been running in the egg-and-spoon race. He was winning. But then he tripped and fell over. He landed face first on the egg. The egg broke. Sol ended up with egg on his face. Everyone else laughed. But Sol didn't. He cried.

It had happened a long time ago. But even now Sol could still remember how he had felt. And that was why he wasn't excited. Sports Day brought back bad memories for him.

"Penny for your thoughts, Sol?" said Mr Reed. He could tell that Sol was worried about something.

"Pardon?" said Sol.

"Is there something you'd like to share with the class?" said Mr Reed.

Sol shook his head. "Not really," he said.

"Are you sure?" said Mr Reed.

Sol nodded. It was bad enough just *thinking* about the time he tripped and got egg on his face. The last thing he wanted to do was to remind everyone else!

"OK," said Mr Reed. "In that case, we need to start planning!"

"Planning?" said Abdul. "Planning what?"

"Sports Day!" said Lou.

"Oh, right," said Abdul.

Samir put his hand up. "Excuse me, Mr Reed," he said.

"Yes, Samir?" said Mr Reed.

"Can grown-ups come and watch?" Samir spoke in a soft voice. He hadn't been at Wigley Primary for very long. He was still a bit shy.

Mr Reed smiled. "Of course they can, Samir," he said.

Samir looked pleased. Noodle licked his hand. It tickled, so Samir laughed.

Marty put his hand up. "Excuse me, Mr Reed," he said.

"Yes, Marty?" said Mr Reed.

"Can Daniel come too?" Marty asked.

"Daniel?" said Mr Reed.

Marty nodded. "Daniel the spaniel," he said.

"Of course!" laughed Mr Reed. He had forgotten that Marty had a puppy. Which was amazing. Because Marty hadn't always liked dogs. Or at least he didn't *think* he liked them. But then Noodle the doodle had joined the class and Marty had soon changed his mind. Now

Marty loved dogs so much that he had one of his very own!

"As long as Daniel doesn't poo everywhere!" said Shakira.

"Can my grandpa come and watch, Mr Reed?" asked Josh.

Mr Reed smiled. "Of course he can, Josh," he said.

"As long as he doesn't poo everywhere," said Sol.

Everyone laughed. Even Mr Reed.

"WOOF!" said Noodle. "WOOF! WOOF! WOOF!"

"Ah, yes," said Mr Reed. "Thank you for reminding me, Noodle. There's something else I need to tell you."

The pupils all looked at Mr Reed. What was he about to say?

"This year," said Mr Reed, "it's going to be an *alternative* Sports Day!"

CHAPTER 2
Sol's Secret

"An alternative Sports Day?" said Abdul.

"What does that mean?" asked Callum.

"It means it's going to be different," said Lou.

"Exactly," said Mr Reed. "Thank you, Lou."

"How is Sports Day going to be different, Mr Reed?" asked Nora.

"Good question, Nora," said Mr Reed. "It's going to be *different* because we're going to try to think of some brand-new events."

"Cool," said Marty.

"So?" said Mr Reed. "Any ideas?"

Josh put his hand up.

"Yes, Josh?" said Mr Reed.

"How about an egg-and-spoon race?" said Josh.

"NOOOOO!" yelled Sol.

"WOOF! WOOF! WOOF!" said Noodle the doodle, and hid under Samir's seat. The noise had scared him.

Samir reached down and stroked Noodle. "It's OK, boy," he said.

Everyone stared at Sol. What was the matter? Why had he shouted like that?

"What's up?" said Callum.

Sol didn't want to say what was wrong.

"Nothing," said Sol. "I just don't like eggs, that's all."

"You don't have to *eat* them, Sol!" said Nora.

Everyone laughed. Even Sol. His secret was safe for now.

"An egg-and-spoon race is a good idea, Josh," said Mr Reed. "But how about something *more* alternative? A bit *more* different?"

"An *orange*-and-spoon race?" said Abdul.

"An *onion*-and-spoon race?" said Marty.

Shakira grinned. "What about a macaroni-cheese-and-spoon race?" she said.

13

Everyone laughed again.

"Any ideas *apart* from carrying things on spoons?" said Mr Reed.

Lou put her hand up.

"Yes, Lou?" said Mr Reed.

"How about Book Balancing?" said Lou.

Abdul turned to Lou. "*Book* Balancing?" he said.

"Yes," said Lou. "Running with a book balanced on your head!"

"That's a great idea!" said Josh.

"And then afterwards we can all sit down and have a read," said Lou.

"Even better!" said Mr Reed. He picked up a marker pen and wrote "Book Balancing" on the white board. "Excellent, Lou. Any other ideas?"

Callum put his hand up.

"Yes, Callum?" said Mr Reed.

"Speed Dressing?" said Callum.

No one said anything. Everyone looked puzzled. So Callum explained.

"You have to run. Then stop and put something on. Then run a bit more and then stop and put something else on. Then run a bit more and ..."

"Then stop and put something else on," said Shakira. She laughed. "Yeah, we get it, Callum!"

Sol grinned. "You should be pretty good at that, Callum!" he said.

"Why?" said Callum.

"Because you always look like you got dressed in a hurry!" said Sol.

Everyone laughed. Even Callum. Because it was true. He always got up late and had to hurry to put his clothes on.

"Speed Dressing," said Mr Reed, writing it on the white board. "I like it. Good idea, Callum."

Callum smiled. If there was a prize for Speed Dressing, he was sure to win it. But what would the prize be?

"Anyone else?" said Mr Reed. "We just need a couple more ideas."

"I've got a Frisbee," said Abdul.

"Congratulations," laughed Sol. "My grandma's got a caravan!"

"Huh?" said Abdul. "I mean we could throw it."

"Ooh yes!" said Nora. "And the one who throws the Frisbee the furthest is the winner!"

"Cool," said Marty.

Mr Reed wrote down "Frisbee Throwing" on the white board. "Very good, Abdul," he said.

"Sorry, Abdul," said Sol. "I just thought you were being weird!"

Abdul smiled. "That's OK," he said.

"One more idea?" said Mr Reed.

"Hey, what about football?" said Josh.

Shakira rolled her eyes. "Not *everyone* likes football, Josh!" she said.

Josh grinned. "Not *everyone* likes macaroni cheese!" he said.

Shakira looked shocked. "Really?" she said.

Samir put his hand up. He had just remembered something. Something they used

to do on Sports Day at his old school. But was
it *different*?

Mr Reed smiled. "Yes, Samir?" he said. "Do
you have an idea?"

Samir nodded. He felt shy. Everyone was
staring at him. Would they think his idea
was silly?

"WOOF!" said Noodle. He looked up at Samir. Noodle wagged his tail and began to pant. His tongue stuck out of his mouth. It looked like a piece of pink ham.

Lou smiled. "I think he wants you to tell us what your idea is, Samir," she said.

Samir looked around. "We could have a Tug of War," he said. His voice was even softer than usual.

"A *what?*" said Abdul.

"Tug of War," said Samir. By now his voice was almost a whisper. He wished he hadn't said anything.

Callum turned to Abdul. "Don't you know what that is?" he said. "You get a big bit of rope. And one team holds one end and another team holds the other end. And then they try to pull each other over a line."

Abdul smiled. "I know what it is," he said. "I just think it's the best idea ever!"

"So do I!" said Shakira.

"Me too!" said Lou.

"Yeah!" said Josh. "Nice one, Samir!"

"Yes, well done, Samir," said Mr Reed. "That's a very good idea indeed!"

Samir smiled as Mr Reed wrote "Tug of War" on the white board.

"WOOF!" said Noodle the doodle. "WOOF! WOOF! WOOF! WOOF! WOOF!"

Samir reached down and stroked Noodle. "Good boy," he said.

CHAPTER 3
Teams

It had been decided. There would be four different events at Sports Day. Book Balancing, Speed Dressing, Frisbee Throwing and Tug of War. Everyone was very excited as they spilled out into the playground for morning break.

Noodle whizzed about like crazy. His tail was wagging faster than ever. His tongue was flapping around like a flag. The only time Noodle stopped was to pee on a tree.

"I'm glad *I'm* not a tree," said Abdul to Josh.

They were both watching Noodle. He was still peeing.

Josh laughed. "That's the weirdest thing I've ever heard," he said.

"Well, can you imagine?" said Abdul.

"Being a tree?" laughed Josh. "No, I really can't."

Nora was looking up at the sky. "I hope it's like this next Friday," she said.

Marty looked puzzled. "Like what?" he said.

"Nice weather," said Nora.

"Oh," said Marty. "I see what you mean. Yes. That would be good, wouldn't it?"

Nora was right. It was a beautiful day. The sun was shining. It wasn't too hot. It wasn't too cold. There was no wind. There was no rain. It was perfect weather for Sports Day.

The bell rang. It was time to go back inside. Back in the classroom, Mr Reed was waiting for all the children to sit down.

"OK, everyone," he said. "We need to speak about teams."

Callum looked puzzled. "Teams?" he said.

"Yeah," said Josh. "Like in football."

"I know what *teams* are, Josh," said Callum. "I just thought we'd all be competing against each other."

Mr Reed looked around. "What do you think, everyone?" he said. "Teams? Or no teams?"

"Teams," said Marty.

"Teams," said Lou.

"Teams," said Nora.

Mr Reed turned to Sol. "What about you, Sol?" he said. "Teams, or no teams?"

Sol remembered the egg-and-spoon race again. He hated the thought of something embarrassing happening at this Sports Day. But if it did, perhaps it would be best to be part of a team. And if he was part of a team, they might even win!

Mr Reed could tell that he was thinking about something. "Well, Sol?" he said.

"Teams," said Sol.

Mr Reed waited to see if anyone else was going to say anything. But no one did.

"Right," said Mr Reed. "Teams it is then."

"Boys against girls?" said Abdul.

"That wouldn't be fair!" said Lou.

"You're right," said Shakira, grinning. "It *wouldn't* be fair. On the *boys*!"

Shakira and Lou laughed and high-fived.

"I know," said Josh. "How about me on one team – and everyone else on the other team?"

Callum turned to Josh. "You're not serious, are you?" he asked.

"Maybe," said Josh. But he was smiling when he said it.

"WOOF! WOOF! WOOF!" said Noodle the Doodle.

"What's that, Noodle?" said Mr Reed. "There have to be three teams?"

"WOOF! WOOF! WOOF!" said Noodle again. He wagged his tail three times. It thumped on the floor.

Callum was looking confused. "Three teams?" he said. "Why?"

"Well, there are nine of us," said Nora. "So we can't have two teams. Because that would mean five on one side and four on the other."

"Oh, right," said Callum.

"And that really *wouldn't* be fair," said Abdul.

"Exactly," said Nora. "So we should have three teams of three instead."

Mr Reed smiled.

"Well done, Nora!" he said.

"WOOF!" said Noodle. "WOOF! WOOF! WOOF!"

Mr Reed laughed. "And well done, Noodle!" he said. "What would we do without you?"

Noodle wagged his tail. He felt very happy. And very important too.

"So, how are we going to choose the teams, Mr Reed?" said Marty.

"Hmm," said Mr Reed. "That's a very good question, Marty."

"WOOF!" said Noodle. "WOOF! WOOF! WOOF!"

"What's that, Noodle?" said Mr Reed. "We should take it in turns to pick coloured counters out of a bag?"

"WOOF!" said Noodle. His tail wagged even faster.

"That's an excellent idea," said Mr Reed.

They put nine coloured counters in a bag. Three were red, three were blue and three were yellow. Then the children took turns to pick

one out. Shakira, Abdul and Josh all picked red counters. So they were in the Red Team. Marty, Lou and Callum all picked blue counters. So they were in the Blue Team. And Sol, Samir and Nora all picked yellow counters. So they were in the Yellow Team.

*

The sun was still shining when it was time for afternoon break. The children ran into the playground. Noodle whizzed around and then peed on the tree.

"Let's go!" said Lou.

Everyone stopped what they were doing and looked at Lou. Even Noodle stopped whizzing about and sat down. He was panting like a steam train.

"Go where?" said Abdul.

"Nowhere," said Lou.

"Huh?" said Callum. "What do you mean?"

"We need to start training!" said Lou.

"*Training?*" said Shakira, as if Lou had just suggested a school trip to the Moon.

"Of course," said Lou. "What's wrong with that?"

"Yeah, what's wrong with that, Shakira?" said Sol.

"What's wrong with it?" laughed Shakira. "It's a school Sports Day – not the Olympics!"

Sol shrugged. "So?" he said.

"Fail to prepare – prepare to fail," said Samir.

Everyone turned to look at him. They hadn't expected him to say anything like that.

"That's what my mum says, Samir!" said Callum. "Fail to prepare – prepare to fail!"

"WOOF!" said Noodle. "WOOF! WOOF! WOOF!"

Noodle wagged his tail and gave Samir's hand a lick. Samir smiled and stroked Noodle's head.

"It's true," said Josh. "Even the best footballers still have to train!"

"Exactly!" said Lou. "So what are we waiting for?"

Shakira sighed. "Whatever," she said.

Josh began walking away.

"Come on, Shakira," Josh said. "You too, Abdul."

"Huh?" said Abdul.

"We're on the same team," said Josh. "We need to train together."

"Oh, right," said Abdul.

Lou started walking to a different part of the playground. "Blue team. This way!" she said.

Marty and Callum followed after Lou.

"Hang on," said Nora.

Everyone turned to look at her.

"We need equipment," said Nora.

"Equipment?" said Marty.

Nora nodded. "To train with," she said.

"Good point, Nora," said Lou. "We need books to balance on our heads."

"Yeah," said Callum. "And more clothes to put on."

"And a Frisbee," said Abdul.

"And some rope," said Samir.

"Yeah," said Sol. "How can we train for the Tug of War if we don't have any rope?"

But before anyone could say anything else, the bell rang. That meant it was the end of break. They had spent so long *talking* about training that there was no time left to *do* any training. They would have to wait until tomorrow now. Everyone was disappointed. Well, *nearly* everyone.

Shakira seemed pleased. "What a *shame*," she said, grinning as everyone began heading back into class.

Sol stared at her. He knew that she wasn't being serious.

"Hey, *you* might not want to win, Shakira," said Sol. "But *I* do!"

"WOOF!" said Noodle. "WOOF! WOOF! WOOF!"

Everyone turned around. Noodle was having one last pee on the tree.

"It's a pity there's not a peeing event at Sports Day," said Abdul. "Because Noodle would definitely win that!"

"Easy-*peasy!*" grinned Sol.

"Ha!" said Josh. "Good one, Sol!"

CHAPTER 4

Come Back with that Frisbee!

The next day was Friday. As soon as it was time for morning break, the children rushed outside. They were full of energy and ready to train again. Sports Day was only a week away.

Each team practised different events. Lou, Marty and Callum began by balancing books on top of their heads. Then they walked around the playground. They walked slowly at first in case the books fell off. But at last they started to run.

Noodle ran after them. He was very excited. His tail was wagging. His tongue was flapping like a piece of pink ham.

"WOOF!" said Noodle. "WOOF! WOOF! WOOF!"

"Watch out, Noodle!" yelled Lou. "You're going to trip me up!"

"WOOF!" said Noodle. "WOOF! WOOF! WOOF!"

Callum laughed. "I think he wants to read your book, Lou!" he said.

"Ha!" said Marty. "Dogs are clever. But they're not *that* clever!"

Nora, Sol and Samir appeared carrying a big basket from the drama cupboard. It was full of clothes and fancy-dress costumes. But the basket was heavy. So after a few steps they put it down on the ground.

Noodle spotted the basket straight away and whizzed towards it. He sniffed the basket and lifted his leg to pee.

"No, Noodle!" said Samir in a stern voice. Noodle seemed to understand because he whizzed over to the tree and peed on that instead.

Marty had been watching. "Wow, Samir!" he said. "That was amazing! Daniel never listens to me. He pees and poos *everywhere*!"

"Aw!" said Lou. "But Daniel is just a puppy!"

"Hmm," said Marty. "I suppose so."

Sol tipped the clothes out of the basket. He and Nora began sorting them into piles. Samir looked around to see where Noodle was. But there was no need to worry. Noodle was already trotting towards Abdul, Shakira and Josh. Because, like most dogs, Noodle the doodle was very nosy. He liked to know what was going on.

Abdul had brought his own Frisbee from home. It was silver and shiny. It sparkled in the sunshine.

"Ready?" Abdul said.

"Ready," said Josh and Shakira together.

"OK," said Abdul. "Here goes."

Abdul threw the Frisbee as hard as he could. It flew across the playground like a flying saucer.

"Whoa!" said Shakira. "That's really cool, Abdul."

"Yeah!" said Josh. "Awesome!"

"WOOF! WOOF! WOOF!" said Noodle.

The children watched as Noodle set off after the Frisbee like a small furry rocket.

"NOOOOODLE!" yelled Abdul. "NOOOOOOOO!"

But it was too late. Before the Frisbee had even landed, Noodle jumped in the air and caught it in his mouth.

"My Frisbee!" wailed Abdul.

"Don't worry, Abdul," said Josh. "I'll get it back for you!"

Josh began running towards Noodle. But Noodle thought it was all part of the game. His tail started wagging like crazy. Just before Josh reached him, Noodle set off again. Josh was a very fast runner. But Noodle was even faster.

Noodle the doodle whizzed around the playground with the Frisbee in his mouth.

"OI! NOODLE!" yelled Josh. "Come back with that Frisbee!"

But it was no good. Noodle didn't come back. He just kept whizzing around faster and faster.

"Come on, everyone!" yelled Josh. "HELP ME!"

All the children began chasing after Noodle. Well, *nearly* all of them.

Samir stood in the middle of the playground. He put two fingers in his mouth and blew. It made a loud whistling sound. Noodle stopped whizzing straight away. He looked at Samir. Everyone else stopped and looked at Noodle. What would he do now?

"Sit," said Samir.

Noodle the doodle sat down on the ground.

Samir looked at Noodle and held one hand up. He looked like a police officer controlling traffic. But Samir wasn't controlling traffic. He was controlling a dog.

"Stay," said Samir.

Noodle stayed where he was and Samir walked up to him.

"Drop it," said Samir.

A second later, Noodle dropped the Frisbee.

"Good boy," said Samir. He gave Noodle a stroke. Then Samir picked the Frisbee up and took it to Abdul.

"Here you are, Abdul," said Samir.

Samir held out the Frisbee. It was covered in dog drool.

"Aw, yuck!" Abdul said. "It's all wet and yucky!"

The others all turned and looked at Abdul.

"Erm, I mean thank you, Samir," Abdul said, and took the Frisbee. "That was very kind of you."

Samir smiled. "You're welcome," he said.

"WOOF!" said Noodle. "WOOF! WOOF! WOOF!"

"What's that, Noodle?" laughed Sol. "You're very sorry and you won't do it again?"

Noodle wagged his tail. His tongue flapped about. Everyone else laughed too. Even Abdul.

CHAPTER 5

Eyes on the Prize

The children trained on Monday too. And on Tuesday and Wednesday. Each time it was Sol who ran out into the playground first. And when the bell rang it was always Sol who went back into class last.

He was determined that nothing embarrassing was going to happen on Sports Day. He wanted to forget all about the egg-and-spoon race when he was younger. He needed to put all that behind him. It was time

to move on. And how was he going to do that?
Simple. By making sure that *his* team won.

"Come on, Yellow Team!" said Sol. "You need
to go much faster than that!"

It was Thursday. The weather was still
beautiful. Nora and Samir were walking around
with books balanced on their heads.

"We're going as fast as we can!" said Nora.
"Isn't that right, Samir?"

Samir didn't say anything. He nodded
instead. The book fell off his head.

"Oops," said Samir.

Josh laughed. He was practising Speed
Dressing with Shakira and Abdul.

Sol turned around and glared. "What's so
funny, Josh?" he said.

"Nothing," said Josh. But he was trying not to grin.

"Where's the fire, Sol?" said Shakira.

Sol turned around to find Shakira smiling at him. She had turned the clothes basket upside down and was sitting on it.

"Huh?" said Sol. "What do you mean, where's the fire? What fire?"

"It's just an expression," said Nora. "It means 'what's the hurry?'"

Sol looked at Shakira. "Do you really not want to win?" he said.

"Not really," said Shakira. She turned to Abdul and Josh. "Sorry, you two."

"That's OK," said Abdul. "I don't mind."

"Huh?" said Josh. He couldn't believe what his teammates were saying. What was the point of taking part in something if you didn't want to win? He wished he were on the same team as Sol! He wished they could swap from one team to another like footballers did!

"Well, I want to win," said Callum.

The Blue Team were practising throwing the Frisbee as far as they could. Or they were *trying* to anyway. But Noodle kept whizzing after it like a small furry rocket. Noodle thought it was the best game ever. So Lou, Marty and Callum threw the Frisbee to each other instead. They had to make sure they grabbed it before Noodle did!

"I want to win too, Callum," said Lou.

"Me too," said Marty. "I wonder what the prize is!"

"Yeah," said Callum. "Me too!"

"YELLOW TEAM! YELLOW TEAM!" yelled Sol.

"BLUE TEAM! BLUE TEAM! BLUE TEAM!" sang Callum, Marty and Lou together.

"WOOF!" said Noodle the doodle. "WOOF! WOOF! WOOF!"

Noodle whizzed around from one team to another. His tail was wagging like crazy. His tongue was flapping about like a slice of wet ham.

"What's that, Noodle?" laughed Shakira. "You think everyone needs to chill out and that winning is for losers?"

"That's not what Noodle's saying," said Samir. But he said it so softly that only his two teammates heard him.

"What was that, Samir?" said Josh. "Speak up."

Everything went quiet in the playground. Noodle had stopped whizzing around. Samir was looking at his feet. He knew that everyone was staring at him. He felt very shy.

Nora looked at Samir and smiled.

"It's OK, Samir," she said. "What do you think Noodle was trying to say?"

Samir looked up and spoke. "He says he wants *everyone* to win. Isn't that right, Noodle?"

"WOOF!" said Noodle the doodle. "WOOF! WOOF! WOOF!"

"AAAAAAAAAAAAAW!" sang all the other children. Even Shakira.

There was a low, rumbling sound.

"What was that?" said Marty.

"My stomach!" laughed Shakira.

"I think it was thunder," said Nora.

"Thunder?" said Callum.

"Look," said Abdul. He was pointing in the direction that the sound had come from.

Everyone looked. The sky was getting darker. The branches of the tree in the playground began to move. It wasn't as warm as before.

"I think it's going to rain," said Lou.

"Oh yeah?" said Shakira. "In that case we'd better get cracking."

Everyone turned to look at Shakira. She stood up and turned the clothes basket the right way around.

"Well?" Shakira said. "What are we waiting for? It's Sports Day tomorrow, isn't it? We need to do some more training!"

Sol and Shakira looked at each other. Sol gave Shakira a thumbs-up. It looked like she *did* want to win after all.

"WOOF!" said Noodle, whizzing around again. "WOOF! WOOF! WOOF!"

CHAPTER 6

New Pup on the Block

It rained all night. And it was still raining when school began the next day.

"Good morning, everyone!" said Mr Reed.

"Goooood mooooooorning, Mis-ter Reeeeeeed!" sang the children. They stretched out each word like they always did. But it wasn't as loud as normal. Everyone sounded a bit sad.

"WOOF!" said Noodle the doodle. But even Noodle's woof wasn't as loud as normal. And his tail wasn't wagging. It was as if he knew what

everyone else was thinking. Would Sports Day
have to be cancelled because of the weather?
They'd all been looking forward to it so much.
Even Shakira.

"Don't worry," Mr Reed said. "It's going to be
nice this afternoon."

"Are you sure, Mr Reed?" Nora said.

Mr Reed smiled.

"I'm sure, Nora," he said. "I've had a look at the weather forecast. The rain is going to stop very soon."

"Fingers crossed," said Abdul.

Lou nodded. "Yes," she said. "And toes."

"WOOF!" said Noodle. "WOOF! WOOF!"

"What's that, Noodle?" said Marty. "Paws crossed too?"

The others turned and looked at Noodle. He was lying on the floor. One of his front paws was crossed over the other.

"Aw," said Shakira. "So cute!"

Samir reached down and tickled Noodle's tummy. Noodle rolled onto his back and stretched out his legs.

"Hey, look!" said Josh. He was pointing out of the window. "I think the rain is stopping now!"

Everyone else turned and looked out of the window too. Josh was right. The rain really did seem to be stopping. Everything was going to be OK after all. Sports Day would go ahead as planned.

Mr Reed smiled. "See?" he said. "I told you!"

"YEEEEEEEEEEEAAAAAAAAAAH!" sang Mr Reed's pupils all together.

"WOOF!" said Noodle the doodle. "WOOF! WOOF! WOOF! WOOF! WOOF!"

*

They set off after lunch. Everyone walked from school to the park. They were all excited. There was lots of chatting and laughing.

"YELLOW TEAM! YELLOW TEAM!" sang Nora, Sol and Samir.

"BLUE TEAM! BLUE TEAM!" sang Marty, Lou and Callum.

"RED TEAM! RED TEAM!" sang Josh, Shakira and Abdul.

"WOOF! WOOF! WOOF!" said Noodle the doodle.

Noodle was trotting along with the children. Samir was holding his lead. Noodle's tail was wagging at full speed. His tongue was flapping like a flag. It looked as if he was smiling.

"Good boy," said Samir.

"WOOF!" said Noodle. "WOOF! WOOF! WOOF!"

Noodle loved going to the park. There were always new things to sniff. There were always people to say hello to. And, best of all, there were always squirrels to chase. But no one minded because Noodle never caught one. Squirrels were much too fast. And they could climb trees. But that didn't stop him from trying. Nothing would ever stop Noodle the doodle from trying to catch a squirrel!

It wasn't far from the school to the park. It only took a few minutes to get there. A crowd of people had already arrived. Mums and dads. Younger brothers and sisters. Grandmas and grandpas. Aunts and uncles. Everyone wanted to watch Wigley Primary Sports Day. And now it was time for it to begin!

The first event was Book Balancing. One person from each team stood at the start line. Shakira from the Red Team. Marty from the Blue Team. Sol from the Yellow Team. All three of them put a book on their heads.

"On your marks!" called Mr Reed. "Get set! Go!"

Shakira, Marty and Sol began walking as fast as they could.

"COME ON, SHAKIRA!" yelled Abdul and Josh.

"COME ON, MARTY!" yelled Lou and Callum.

"COME ON, SOL!" yelled Nora and Samir.

"WOOF! WOOF! WOOF!" said Noodle the doodle.

But at that moment there was another barking sound. And it didn't sound anything like Noodle. Noodle's bark was deep like the low notes on a piano. This bark was more like a squeak. Like one of the high notes on a piano.

Everyone turned around to see a tiny black dot charging across the park towards them.

"Oh no," said Marty. The book on his head wobbled and fell off. Marty knew what the black dot was. It was Daniel. Daniel the spaniel.

"DANIEL!" yelled Marty at the top of his voice. "STAY!"

But it was too late. Daniel had already spotted Noodle. And Noodle had already spotted Daniel. Daniel was just a puppy. He didn't know what "stay" meant. He only wanted to play.

"WOOF!" squeaked Daniel the spaniel. "WOOF! WOOF! WOOF!"

"WOOF!" said Noodle the doodle. "WOOF! WOOF! WOOF!"

Noodle shot forward. But Samir was holding his lead. So Samir shot forward too. He tried pulling on the lead. But Noodle was too strong and Samir had to let go.

"LOOK OUT, SOL!" yelled Nora as Noodle and Daniel began chasing each other around and around.

But it was too late.

Noodle's lead had got tangled up around Sol's feet. Sol did his best to carry on. But the book fell off his head. Then he tripped and fell over.

Sol lay on the ground. He couldn't believe what had happened. It was just like that time long ago. When he'd tripped and got egg on his face and everyone had laughed. Yellow Team had trained so hard for this. And now he'd messed things up!

"Are you OK, Sol?" said Lou.

Everyone was looking at him. But no one was laughing. They were worried about their friend.

"What?" said Sol. "Erm, yeah. I'm fine, thanks."

"It wasn't your fault," said Abdul.

"It was an accident," said Nora.

"WOOF!" said Noodle. "WOOF! WOOF! WOOF!"

Sol looked at Noodle. He was gazing up at Sol. His tail had stopped wagging. Sol smiled. How could anyone be cross with Noodle the doodle?

"It's OK, boy," said Sol. "I know you didn't mean it."

Noodle jumped up and began licking Sol's face. His tail was wagging like crazy.

"Aw, yuck!" yelled Josh. "That's disgusting!"

"No, it's not!" laughed Marty. "Noodle is just saying sorry!"

"Huh?" said Josh. "No. Not that! *That!*"

Everyone turned around to see Daniel the spaniel doing a poo on the grass.

"Aw, yuck!" laughed Shakira.

Marty's mum was running across the park towards them. "I'm so sorry," she said.

Mr Reed smiled. "It's OK," he said.

"WOOF!" said Noodle. "WOOF! WOOF! WOOF!"

"That's right, Noodle," said Mr Reed. "Dogs will be dogs."

Marty's mum got a poo bag out of her pocket. She picked up the poo and went to find a bin.

CHAPTER 7
Ready, Steady, Throw!

Mr Reed decided not to carry on with the Book Balancing event. He didn't want anyone falling over and hurting themselves. Sports Day was supposed to be fun, not dangerous!

The next event was Speed Dressing. Josh, Nora and Callum lined up next to each other. Ahead of them were three piles of clothes.

"Ready?" said Mr Reed.

"Ready!" said Josh, Nora and Callum all together.

"Excellent," said Mr Reed. "On your marks! Get dressed! Go!"

Josh, Nora and Callum dashed towards the first pile of clothes.

"CALLUM! CALLUM!" yelled Lou and Marty.

"NORA! NORA!" yelled Samir and Sol.

"JOSH! JOSH! JOSH!" yelled Abdul and Shakira.

Callum, Nora and Josh hopped about as they struggled to put on some big trousers over their own clothes. It was very funny.

After that, they ran towards a pile of big coats. Josh and Callum were just about to put one on when Nora spotted something.

"Stop!" she said.

"What is it?" said Callum. He was cross because he wanted to win.

Nora put a finger to her lips. "Sssshhh!" she said. "Look!"

Nora pointed at the pile of coats. Callum and Josh looked.

"Aaaaaaaaw!" said Callum.

"So sweet!" said Josh.

Everyone else ran over to see what they were looking at. Noodle the doodle and Daniel the spaniel had fallen asleep in the coats.

They were cuddled up together in a furry ball.
Noodle had one paw across Daniel. They looked
so warm and cosy. The coats were like a nest.

"AAAAAAAAAAAAAW!" sang everyone
together.

"That is the cutest thing I've ever seen!" said
Shakira.

Marty smiled. "Come on, you," he said, and
picked Daniel up. Noodle stretched out and
made a funny growling sound. He was still
fast asleep. But Daniel woke up. He did a great
big yawn and licked Marty's nose as if it was a
sausage.

"AAAAAAAAAAAAAW!" sang everyone
again. It looked like that was the end of the
Speed Dressing event!

*

The next event was Frisbee Throwing. Abdul was going to throw first because it was his Frisbee.

"Ready ... steady ... throw!" said Mr Reed.

Abdul threw the Frisbee. It flew through the air. On and on it went. The others watched as the Frisbee skimmed over the grass.

"Wow, Abdul!" said Shakira. "That's amazing!"

"RED TEAM! RED TEAM!" chanted Josh.

"NOOOOOOO!" yelled Abdul.

But it was too late. Daniel the spaniel had jumped out of Marty's arms and was charging after the Frisbee as fast as his legs could take him.

Noodle woke up when Abdul shouted. He saw the Frisbee too and set off after it. He shot across the park like a furry bullet. But who would reach the Frisbee first? Daniel the spaniel was fast. But Noodle was even faster.

Daniel and Noodle reached the Frisbee at exactly the same time. They grabbed it with their mouths. They both began to pull. They whizzed around in circles. Then Noodle growled and Daniel let go.

Everyone watched and waited. Would Noodle run away with the Frisbee?

Samir put two fingers in his mouth and blew. It made a loud whistling sound. Noodle looked at Samir for a moment and then started running towards him. His tail was wagging like a windscreen wiper. Noodle's mouth was full of Frisbee, but it still looked like he was smiling.

Noodle stopped in front of Samir.

"Good boy," said Samir. "Sit."

Noodle sat.

"Drop it," said Samir.

Noodle dropped the Frisbee. Samir picked it up and gave it to Abdul.

"Thanks, Samir," said Abdul.

"WOOF!" said Noodle the doodle.

Abdul grinned. "Sorry," he said. "I meant, thanks, *Noodle!*"

Everyone laughed. Well, *nearly* everyone. Mr Reed was looking up at the sky. Clouds were rolling towards them. It had suddenly gone very dark.

"Oh dear," said Mr Reed. "This doesn't look good."

Mr Reed was right. A moment later there was a low rumbling sound in the distance.

"Thunder," said Nora.

"Oh no," said Sol. "Not now!"

CHAPTER 8
We Won't Bite!

"I think we'd better call it a day," said Mr Reed.

The children all turned and looked at him.

"You mean go back to school, Mr Reed?" said Lou.

"I'm afraid so, Lou," said Mr Reed.

Everyone looked shocked. They had all trained so hard. They couldn't give up now.

"What?" said Sol. "We can't do that!"

"I'm very sorry, Sol," said Mr Reed. "But we can't take any risks."

"Risks?" said Shakira.

Mr Reed nodded. "Correct, Shakira," he said. "It looks like there's a storm heading this way. We're going to get soaked if we stay out here much longer."

"And we might get struck by lightning," said Nora.

Everyone turned to look at Nora. No one had thought about that. Until now.

"I mean it probably *won't* happen," said Nora. "But you never know."

"Indeed, Nora," said Mr Reed. "Better safe than sorry."

"But ..." began Samir. He stopped again. He felt very shy.

"What is it, Samir?" said Mr Reed.

Samir stared at the ground. "What about Tug of War?" he said.

"Yes," said Josh. "And what about prizes?"

Mr Reed smiled at Josh. "Prizes, Josh?" he said.

Josh nodded. "For the winners!" he said.

Mr Reed laughed. "Who said anything about *prizes*?" he said. "Because I didn't!"

Everyone looked at Mr Reed. Was he being serious? Or was he joking? It was hard to tell. But they were all disappointed. No one wanted to go back to school yet.

"Please, Mr Reed?" said Samir.

Mr Reed looked around. The sky was getting even darker.

"I don't think we have enough time, Samir," he said. "There are three teams. It would take too long for everyone to take part."

They all thought for a moment.

"What if there were just *two* teams?" said Marty.

"Yes!" said Callum. "Then it wouldn't take so long! Good idea, Marty!"

"Hmm," said Nora. "There's just one problem."

"What's that?" said Shakira.

"Two into nine doesn't go," said Nora.

"Huh?" said Shakira.

"There are nine of us," said Nora. "That means there would have to be five on one side and four on the other."

"And the old teams would be all mixed up," said Abdul.

"That doesn't matter," said Mr Reed.

The children looked at Mr Reed.

"So we can do it then?" said Sol.

Mr Reed thought for a moment and then smiled. "OK," he said. "But we have to be very quick."

"YEEEEEEEEEEEEAAAAAAAAAAH!" yelled all the children.

"WOOF!" said Noodle. "WOOF! WOOF! WOOF!"

"OK, everyone!" said Mr Reed. "Get into two teams now! And hurry!"

Everyone looked at each other for a second and then formed two groups. The boys were in one group and the girls in the other.

"That's not right," said Josh. "There are six of us but only three of you."

Sol smiled. The teams might be mixed up but he still wanted to win.

"It seems OK to me!" he said.

"You can come and join us if you want, Josh?" said Lou.

"Yeah, come on, Josh," said Shakira. "We won't bite!"

Shakira, Lou and Nora laughed.

Josh thought for a moment. He was good at sports. He didn't care which team he was on.

"OK," he said. "Whatever."

Josh walked over and joined the girls. Now there were five on one team and four on the other.

"Well done, Josh," said Mr Reed. "Let's get cracking!"

CHAPTER 9
Everyone's a Winner

There was a long piece of rope on the ground. Sol, Callum, Marty, Abdul and Samir stood in a line at one end. Lou, Nora, Shakira and Josh stood in a line at the other end. A red ribbon was tied in the middle of the rope. And there was a plastic cone next to each team.

"OK," said Mr Reed. "Pick up the rope."

The two teams bent down and picked up the rope.

"Good," said Mr Reed. "Now when I say 'pull', you pull as hard as you can. If you pull the ribbon past your own team's cone, you win. Is that clear?"

"YEEEEEESSS, MIS-TER REEEEEEEEEEEEEEED!" sang all the children together.

The two teams stared at each other as they waited to pull. They gritted their teeth and dug their heels into the ground. They all wanted to win so much!

"Excellent," said Mr Reed. "On your marks ... get set ... PULL!"

The two teams pulled as hard as they could. First the rope went one way. Then it went the other way. But after a while the team of four began to get tired. The team of five pulled and pulled. It looked like they were going to win.

"COME ON!" yelled Josh to his team-mates. "PULL!"

"What do you *think* we're doing?" yelled Shakira.

"Well, pull harder then!" yelled Josh.

But it was no good. The team of five were just too strong. The red ribbon got closer and closer to their plastic cone. Until ...

"WOOF!" said Noodle the doodle. "WOOF! WOOF! WOOF!"

Everyone watched as Noodle suddenly raced towards the team of four. He grabbed on to

their end of the rope with his mouth and began to pull as hard as he could.

"Good boy, Noodle!" yelled Lou.

"Yeah!" yelled Shakira. "Come on, Noodle! Pull!"

"We can do this!" yelled Nora.

It was so funny to see Noodle joining in that the other team started to laugh. The more they laughed the less they were able to pull. The team of four – plus Noodle – gave one last big

pull ... and the team of five slipped on the grass and fell over. As they fell, the ribbon flew past the team of four's cone.

"YEAH!" yelled Josh. "WE WON! WE WON! WE WON! GO RED!

"AND BLUE!" yelled Lou.

"AND YELLOW!" yelled Nora.

"That's not fair!" said Callum. "The grass was wet! We slipped!"

"So?" laughed Shakira. "One member of our team is a dog!"

"WOOF!" said Noodle. "WOOF! WOOF! WOOF!"

"What's that, Noodle?" said Mr Reed. "You think we should call it a draw? I think that's a very good idea!"

"Well, I don't," said Sol. "I think it's a *rubbish* idea. No offence, Mr Reed."

Mr Reed smiled. "None taken, Sol," he said. "But why do you think it's a rubbish idea?"

"Erm," said Sol. He thought for a moment. "I'm not sure. I just think there should be a winner."

"Hmm," said Mr Reed. "Interesting."

The children all looked at Mr Reed. They had a feeling he was about to say something important. And they were right. He was.

"What if I said that you are *all* winners?" said Mr Reed. "And that *everyone* is going to get a prize?"

"YEEEEEEEEEEEEAAAAAAAAAAH!" sang the pupils of Wigley Primary.

"Turn around," Mr Reed told the children.

Everyone turned around and saw that
Shakira's mum had appeared. She was holding
a big tray. On the tray were nine dishes full
of ice cream. Three red. Three blue. And
three yellow.

"Whoa!" said Sol.

"Awesome!" said Josh.

"Yum!" said Shakira.

"Well?" laughed Mr Reed. "What are you waiting for? Eat up – before it starts to rain!"

Shakira, Abdul and Josh each took a dish of red ice cream. Marty, Lou and Callum each took a dish of blue ice cream. And Sol, Samir and Nora each took a dish of yellow ice cream.

"Thanks, Shakira's mum!" said Sol, and everyone laughed.

But before anyone could start eating the ice cream, there was a barking sound. Not a deep barking sound. It was more like a squeak. Everyone turned to see Daniel the spaniel whizzing towards them. He grabbed the rope in his mouth and began to pull.

Noodle grabbed the other end of the rope and started pulling too.

"Ha!" said Shakira. "Noodle and Daniel are having their very own Tug of War!"

"More like a *dog* of war!" said Marty.

"On your *barks*!" grinned Sol. "Get set! Pull!"

Everyone laughed again. Noodle let go of the rope. Daniel the spaniel fell over.

"WOOF!" said Noodle the doodle. "WOOF! WOOF! WOOF! WOOF! WOOF!"